Explore God's FOREST

Written and Illustrated by **Michelle Mykowski**

Text and illustrations © 1999 by Michelle Mykowski. Published by The Standard Publishing Company, Cincinnati, Ohio. A division of Standex International Corporation. All rights reserved. Printed in the United States of America. Designed by Rosalie Sherwood Founds. Edited by Laura Ring.

Scripture on page 24 taken from the HOLY BIBLE, NEW INTERNATIONAL VERSION®. NIV®. Copyright © 1973, 1978, 1984 by International Bible Society. Used by permission of Zondervan Publishing House. All rights reserved.

STANDARD PUBLISHING™

06 05 04 03 02 01 00 99   5 4 3 2 1

Library of Congress Catalog Card Number 98-61290
ISBN 0-7847-0900-9

Beyond the busy cities,
a peaceful place can be found.

Let's explore God's forest,

with all its sights and sounds!

The bears curl up for
a long winter's nap.

The den is snug and warm.

God made this cozy cave for them,
a shelter from
the storm.

On the branches above,
the birds nest and sing.

The buds are blooming.
Hooray! It's spring!

Trees provide shade
on a hot summer's day.
Here deer rest

while
chipmunks
play.

the beaver and the moose.

Hear the croaking frog
and the honking goose!

When the leaves change colors,
autumn has begun.

One squirrel works

while another has some fun!

God made every season
and the beauty that we see

To show the love he has
for you and for me!

"For every animal of the forest is mine, and the cattle on a thousand hills. I know every bird in the mountains, and the creatures of the field are mine."

Psalm 50:10, 11